THE
MAGICIAN'S
RING

THE
MAGICIAN'S
RING

Carol Gaskin

illustrations by T. Alexander Price

Library of Congress Cataloging-in-Publication Data

Gaskin, Carol.
   The magician's ring.

   (The Forgotten forest)
   Summary: The reader, as Robin the minstrel, follows
a path of perils through the Forgotten Forest, making
decisions which determine whether he will end up a hero
or a prisoner of thieves.
   1. Plot-your-own stories. 2. Children's stories,
American. [1. Plot-your-own stories. 2. Fantasy]
I. Price, T. Alexander, ill. II. Title. III. Series:
Gaskin, Carol. Forgotten forest.
PZ7.G213Mag 1985 [Fic] 84-8499
ISBN 0-8167-0320-5 (lib. bdg.)
ISBN 0-8167-7598-2 (pbk.)

This edition published in 2003.

Printed in Canada.

10 9 8 7 6 5 4 3 2 1

Welcome to the
Forgotten Forest

In this adventure your name is Robin. A minstrel by trade, you wander far and wide, singing for your supper.

As you read, you will be asked to make important decisions: Will you dine with the Witch of Wandelmere? Will you try to remove the unicorn's ring? Will you enter the Theater of Snakes, or the Tower of Mevar?

There are many paths you can follow in the Forgotten Forest. You may end up trapped in the forest with a ring of thieves—or you may be a hero. The choice is *yours*.

When one adventure ends, you can always return to the beginning and follow a new path. Choose well, and the best of luck in your journey!

You are traveling along a green woodland path, humming happily as you go. The day is sunny and bright, your rucksack feels light on your back, and you expect to reach your destination by nightfall: the wondrous Kingdom of Wandelmere.

You have walked many miles and have had many adventures as a minstrel and teller of tales. You have performed for dukes and dames, viziers and viscounts, and you have supped at the richest of tables. But you have never sung before a king.

You rehearse the new song you have composed to introduce yourself at court.

> *I am a roving troubadour*
> *My name is Minstrel Robin.*
> *I'll sing to you of love and war,*
> *Of wizard, witch, and goblin.*
> *I'll tell the histories of kings,*
> *The mysteries of magic.*
> *A hundred stories I can sing,*
> *Hilarious and tragic.*
> *So if you will, invite me in*
> *And hear the tales of Minstrel Robin!*

You plan to perform your most exciting and noble ballads, and to earn yourself a gourmet meal in the royal banquet hall. Perhaps the king will ask you to set the stories of Wandelmere to music.

Your mouth waters at the thought of royal fare. It is well past noon, so you decide to eat the last bit of bread and cheese in your rucksack. You settle yourself on the side of the path for lunch.

While you eat, you check your few belongings: your precious lute wrapped in a cloth of flannel, a flute you carved with your own hands, your trusty carving knife, a flask of spring water, a flint, a woolen cloak, and three smooth stones you picked up in your travels.

You pack everything neatly back in your rucksack and continue on your way. Birds and an occasional squirrel keep you company, but you meet no other people on the path.

By late afternoon you emerge from the wood. The path joins a much-traveled road, and you begin to think it odd that you haven't met any people. You have heard that Wandelmere is a large kingdom with many subjects and a busy marketplace.

You walk by farms and cottages, mills and dairies. Chickens and geese flock in farmyards, and cows and pigs watch your progress with curiosity. But no one calls a greeting. In the distance you see a great castle rising within the walls of a sprawling town.

You are disturbed. Usually, as soon as you enter a new place, you are surrounded by excited children who herald your arrival in the town. "A minstrel's here! A minstrel!" they cry. In the town square, you sing and play for the townspeople until an invitation is issued from the most noble house. Then in you go to tell your tales. Often you remain for several weeks at a time, singing every night, until you exhaust your supply of stories. The very next day you set out in search of new ones.

It is dusk as you reach the town. The streets are deserted except for two bony dogs who sniff at your feet. Mice scamper by a hungry cat. Curiously, the cat does not chase them.

The dogs trot after you, through twisting streets that lead to the dim castle. In the near darkness, you can see that the drawbridge is lowered and the castle gate is wide open.

You wonder whether to enter the deserted castle or to pitch camp in the empty town for the night. Suddenly candlelight bursts from every window of the castle, and you hear hundreds of voices. Bustle and activity pours forth. Next to you appear two pages, who each grab one of your hands and urge you across the drawbridge.

"Minstrel, come play for our king and courtiers! We crave news of the world, and need your good cheer. Come, Minstrel, sing and play!"

You allow them to lead you into the enormous castle. It is a shambles. Straw covers the floor, and leaves and twigs line the stairs. Berry-stained tapestries lie in crumpled heaps amid littered nutshells. The open helmet on a standing suit of armor reveals a bird's nest, and cobwebs stretch from statues' heads to chandeliers. Servants dart here and there, ignoring the mess.

The two pages lead you to a vast banquet hall. You gasp in awe. Here is all the splendor you expected. Handsome lords and beautiful ladies sit at a banquet table set with platters of silver and gold. A fire burns in a huge hearth, and you smell something delicious being cooked.

At the very end of the long table, enthroned above the courtiers, sit the King and Queen of Wandelmere. They are glorious. You have never seen a nobleman so dashing, nor a lady so lovely, and both smile kindly as you enter. Then the dark-eyed queen makes a gesture of welcome, while the fair-haired king thoughtfully strokes his beard.

The court grows silent, and all eyes stare hopefully at you. Bowing with a flourish to the rulers and courtiers of Wandelmere, you withdraw your lute from your rucksack and perform your new composition.

"Well, Minstrel Robin," says the king when you finish, "we are pleased to have your company. Won't you join us for a meal? Then we shall hear your tales, and I daresay we can tell you one better, though perhaps a bit sad. What say you, my courtiers?"

The lords and ladies excitedly agree. You bow deeply once again, and are led to a seat at the table. You are surprised and not a little disappointed when dinner in this fine hall turns out to be scrambled eggs and applesauce, but you eat hungrily. After dinner, you sing and play and sing some more, until your throat is dry and your eyelids droop. It must be just an hour short of dawn and you are exhausted.

"Whoa, Minstrel Robin!" says the king. "Your tales are marvels, but I see you grow weary. Now you shall hear the strange truth about Wandelmere."

You gratefully lower your lute to listen. The king takes his queen's hand and begins to speak.

"Once, not long ago, ours was a great kingdom. Our labors were fruitful, our food was plentiful, and our people were happy and beautiful.

"There came to Wandelmere a magician, Mevar by name. He was fearsome and wore many disguises. But we had never turned away any guest, and we welcomed Mevar at court. He asked that we share our bounty with him, which we did willingly. But Mevar was not satisfied. He claimed that we were happy because we were beautiful, and he demanded that we give him some of our beauty.

"We tried to explain that we were beautiful because we were happy, and not the other way around. But he would not listen. 'Then I shall take your beauty from you!' he cried."

The king sighs sadly. "We have been enchanted ever since."

"Enchanted in what way, Your Majesty?" you ask.

The king's voice is heavy as he answers. "By day, Mevar has stolen our beauty. And every day we must spend our lives as animals. We resume our true forms only at night, as you see us now. Mevar has enchanted every person in the Kingdom of Wandelmere, except for one crone who comes each morning to tend to our needs.

"Our lives are simple. By day we sleep or forage for food. By night we gather here for comfort. We cannot run the farms or the mills, so our crops have gone to ruin. We eat no meat for fear of harming one of our own. And we do not leave Wandelmere, lest we be harmed by others. We fear that come winter, we will starve. Only a brave outsider can help us. I will reward you well if you can find Mevar and end our sorry predicament."

"I will be honored to help you, Sire," you reply. "And I will begin my search at once. Only tell me, Your Majesty, is there no way to break this wicked spell?"

"Mevar has a ring—" begins the king.

But before your eyes, the lords and ladies, servants and pages fade and disappear, and the banquet hall is filled with animals of every size and shape. The king has become a bearded goat, his queen a graceful doe. There are sheep and sheepdogs, spiders and hares, a weasel, a shrew, a fox and a bear, and many chickens, cows, and pigs.

Now you understand why the courtiers fear to leave Wandelmere. They have been transformed into almost every animal you can think of, and all are animals that are hunted, or stepped on, or trapped, or kept as pets.

The enchanted courtiers file past you out the grand doors of the banquet hall, to their beds, nests, and stalls. You also leave the castle.

You walk by a line of animals waiting on the drawbridge to be fed. You see an ancient crone hobbling toward the castle, pulling a cartload of apples and nuts. She has few teeth, and fewer hairs, but her cheeks are a rosy red. As you approach, she begins to cackle.

"I'm the only one left, Minstrel," she says. "Too ugly for Mevar to change, eh, eh, eh. I tend the animals now, eh, eh. But I know Mevar's secrets, I do—"

She is interrupted by a frantic galloping on the drawbridge. A magnificent dark-red horse leaps by you and blocks your path. He nuzzles your shoulder and pulls on your sleeve. He wants you to go with him.

The crone reaches for the horse in alarm, but he sidesteps away.

"If you take that horse, I'll tell you nothing!" she cries. You wonder if the horse is a member of the royal court.

"Who is he?" you ask.

"I'll tell you nothing," repeats the crone, wagging a crooked finger in your face. "And the king has told you all he knows. But if you come to my cottage tonight, I will tell you what *I* know of the Magician's Ring."

You wonder what to do. You wouldn't want to put the horse in danger, whoever he may be, but he seems to want to go with you. And you don't quite trust the crone, though she seems to know something important.

If you take the horse and ride away, turn to page 36.

If you decide to camp until nightfall and learn the secret of the crone, turn to page 53.

If you leave them both to search for Mevar the Magician alone, turn to page 22.

10

from page 85 / from page 91

You decide to find the trained seals. Making your way around the bleachers, you find the exit that Tamerlane took and leave the Big Top.

It is quiet and dark behind the great tent. The cymbals and bass drum and the squeals of the crowd are muffled.

Catching the scent of horses in the air, you soon discover the animal houses. The sound of barking and splashing leads you to the seals. They are cavorting in a shallow, dimly lit pool. The rainbow-colored ring floats in the center.

One of the bewhiskered animals flops toward you and barks in a friendly manner. He is much larger than you would have imagined, as big as you are.

Leaving your rucksack by the side of the pool, you pet his sleek head. When he offers no resistance, you wrap an arm about his neck and wade into the water. The seal pulls you farther into the pool, supported on his back.

You paddle toward the ring. Its colors seem to vibrate and change with the gently lapping water.

Suddenly you are lifted high into the air on the nose of the playful seal! Your body curls into a ball as he tosses you to another of his playmates—and another! You land in the pool with a splash, only to be picked up again and juggled like a child's toy.

As you roll in the air, you can see the Great Tamerlane out of the corner of your eye. He issues a sharp order to the team of seals. In a tumbling blur, you are dropped through the center of the floating ring.

You surface in the pool to find that you have no trouble swimming. You have grown drooping whiskers and sleek, shiny fur. You clap your flippers together in delight and bark like your newfound brothers. You have always wanted to join the circus!

THE END

from page 50

You decide to climb into the pit. There are no handholds nearby, so you circle the balcony until you come to the spot Mevar used. You find his silken rope-ladder stuffed behind a stalagmite. Fastening it to the rocky spike, you let it unfurl into the pit.

The ladder is so fine and delicate you wonder how it will hold your weight. But Mevar had no trouble. Gripping the soft, smooth ropes at the top of the ladder, you climb down the twisted rungs. The silk is surprisingly strong.

Below to your right, the golden ring gleams and beckons. To your left the dragon waits, watching your descent. He does not look friendly. And his mouth is watering.

You look nervously back to the top of the pit. The stalagmite looms above you, craggy and rough. But it is moving! The jagged rock is slowly breathing, in and out, in and out, sawing through the silken ladder as you hang halfway down. This must be Mevar's doing!

You try to scramble back up the ladder, but the silk is too slippery and skims through your hands like mercury.

The ladder snaps! You are falling into the pit! And the dragon is waiting with his jaws wide open.

THE END

14

from page 71

You decide to eavesdrop on the nearby gnomes for a while. You can always sing lullabies later if you change your mind.

"Let's pretend to fall asleep," you whisper to Jian. "Then they'll talk more freely."

The gnomes watch you both closely as you share some apples and nuts from your rucksack. You eat slowly and take your time. Then you spread your cloak in a corner of the cage, your head resting on your knees. You close your eyes.

One by one the guards get bored, and they look your way less frequently.

"Aarggh," sneers one, "they're sleeping like lambs."

"Like lambs to the slaughter, har, har," says another.

"Maybe I'll carve lamb chops from my ringwood tonight," says a third. "Then Mevar can turn them into lamb chops and we can have a feast!"

"Hush, you oaf!" barks a fourth. "They can hear you!" You don't move a muscle.

"Aarggh," sneers the first, "they're sleeping like lambs."

The gnomes fall silent for a few minutes. Then you hear footsteps and a gruff voice you recognize as the bearlike bully's.

"Whose turn is it to carve tonight?"

"Mine," answers gnome number three.

"Here's your ringwood, then," says the bully. You hear a thud as a piece of wood falls to the ground. "Mevar's ordered an elephant this time."

"What does he want with an elephant?" asks the gnome.

"I don't ask questions," growls the bully. "Maybe he wants to start a circus. Just make it."

"One elephant, coming up," says the gnome, and you hear him chipping at a piece of wood. The bully stomps away.

You think about what you heard. Mevar must use the ringwood carvings to work his transformations. Opening your eyes a crack, you look closely at the pile of treasure in the center of the clearing. You can just make out the shapes of some of the statues amid the jewels: a bearded goat, a shrew, a turtle. You think you also see a horse like Jian. There are many other figures as well, all beautifully carved from highly polished wood with circular markings in the grain. Ringwood!

"Robin, do you see them?" whispers Jian.

"The carvings?" you say. "Yes! How do you suppose they work?"

"I think our true forms must be trapped inside them during the day," answers Jian.

You study your surroundings. All but three of the nine gnomes have gone to join the more festive campfires in the clearing. One guard still sits near you, quietly carving, while the other two play a game of knucklebones.

"Are you ready to escape, Princess?" you ask. "I can take care of the guards if you will cut us a door."

"I'm ready!" she answers.

You give Jian your knife and she starts to work on the back of the cage. The noises she makes are disguised by the loud chipping and shaving sounds made by the woodcarver.

Reaching into your sack, you find your three smooth stones. You wait for one of the gnomes to cast the knucklebones on the ground. Then you toss a stone and strike the other gnome squarely in the chest, just as he tips a tankard of brew to his lips.

"Hey, what did you hit me for?" says the drinker.

"I didn't hit you," says his partner. "You're loony!" They play a few turns in suspicious silence. Then you throw the second stone.

"Hey!" cries the drinking gnome. "You're trying to make me miss, you cheater!"

"Loony!"

"Cheat!"

They soon come to blows. The carver stands up to intervene, but you plant your third stone right between his eyes, and he falls to the ground in a daze. The pair of gnomes argue and scrap, push and shove, until they manage to knock each other out. They tumble across the carver-gnome in a heap.

Such behavior seems so normal at a scoundrels' campfire that none of the other groups pays any attention.

"Let's go!" you whisper. You replace your knife in your rucksack and crawl free of the cage. Jian runs ahead of you into the forest.

"Wait there!" you whisper. Sneaking to the gnomes' campfire, you rescue the piece of ringwood the carver had begun to shape, and stuff it into your rucksack. Then you join Jian. You crouch together in the shadows beyond the clearing.

"What now?" she asks. "Should we try the lullabies? Then we could burn the woodcarvings while the crooks are asleep. I think we have to destroy them at night, while our true forms are our own."

"Maybe we should hide and make sure they discover we have escaped," you answer. "Then some of them are sure to scatter to search for us, and we'll have fewer enemies to conquer."

If you try to lull all of the thugs to sleep, turn to page 78.

If you try to trick some members of the ring into leaving the clearing, turn to page 30.

18

from page 94

You decide you must destroy the Ring of Stones. Perhaps you can pull one of the monoliths down. If only the magical unicorn hair is strong enough for your plan!

Slipping to the nearest stone pillar, you wind a strand of the precious hair around the bulky rock and knot it tightly. To your surprise, the ball of hair unwinds in a single thread.

Improving your plan, you move to the next giant stone, and the next, binding each to the last in an unbroken series of loops. The unicorn's hair is so pale and fine it is invisible in the moonlight.

You slow down as you reach the side of the Ring Mevar faces. He continues to chant in his rumbling voice, "*All the power of the Night! All the power of the Night!*"

As the moonlight strikes his face, you freeze. For the Magician's face is that of a ferocious beast, wolfen, with a raven's beak and the spiral horns of a wild ram.

After a time—you are not certain how long—the chill passes. You must hurry, for the moon is rising quickly.

You duck behind pillar after pillar, tossing the dwindling ball of unicorn hair around each, praying that the brilliant flames of Mevar's fire will blind him to your presence in the darkness.

At last *your* ring is complete. Each stone is encircled in unicorn hair, each connected to its monumental neighbor by an invisible thread. The moon is now almost directly above the Ring of Stones.

Finally, you remove the three smooth stones from your rucksack, weighing them in your hand. Taking a deep breath, you hurl the first small stone at the Magician's head. You hit him! "Mevar, the Ring is crumbling!" you shout. "Come out! Come out!"

Mevar whirls around, searching the night, but he cannot see you behind the stone slab. He casts an anxious eye at the rising moon and resumes his chant.

"The hour is mine! The hour is mine!"

You crawl a third of the way around the ring and hurl another stone at his head, calling, "Mevar, the night is wrong! The Ring will fall!"

The Magician snarls and sends the flames of his fire high into the air, bathing the circle in angry red light. But you stand safely behind a towering pillar.

You hurl your last stone with all of your might, screaming, "The Ring is collapsing! Mevar, look out!"

Your tiny missile hits the Magician squarely on the head. With a horrible cry he leaps from the ring of fire and runs toward the outer circle, searching for you among the stones. Just as the moon reaches its peak, a flash of lightning splits the sky and hurtles down to the center of the ring of flames. But Mevar does not receive the blast of power he has invoked. He is hunting for you.

"The Power!" he wails, and runs back to the dying fire. He chants and mumbles, but it is too late. The time is past.

Mevar's cry of anguish turns to rage. He sniffs at the air and turns in your direction. You have been cowering behind a leaning stone, but now you start to run through the brittle grass.

The Magician charges toward you with a terrifying howl. At full speed he hits a strand of unicorn's hair stretched between two pillars and is catapulted back into the middle of the Ring of Stones.

You hear a wrenching groan as the ground begins to shudder. The stone pillars are falling, jarred loose by the force of Mevar's angry charge! Pulled by the unicorn hair and knocked by their neighbors, the monoliths tumble in a chain reaction, like a toppling line of dominoes!

The Ring of Stones collapses with a thunderous roar, raising a thick cloud of dust that begins to settle over the ruin.

Your quest is over. You have destroyed the Magician's Ring.

THE END

from page 9 / from page 44

You wander for many days and nights, leaving Wandelmere far behind you.

You stop in every town and hamlet along the way, singing for your supper and inquiring about the Magician's Ring. The tale you hear is always the same: townsfolk have disappeared. Stories are whispered of people changed into animals. And always the rumors began when a traveling circus was passing through town. But no, no one has heard of a Mevar or his ring.

You are sure there is a connection between the Magician and the strange stories. So, in search of Mevar, you follow the trail of the circus.

At last, one pleasant evening, you catch up to the traveling show. Banners in the streets of a small town proclaim Circus! Come One, Come All! Tonight Only! Men, women, and children are pouring excitedly toward the fairground on the outskirts of town. Calliope music fills the air.

Encircling the fairground are gaily painted circus wagons. A huge, striped tent rises majestically at the center—a canvas castle. All is noise and confusion, and you are jostled along by the happy crowd.

"Hey-a, hey-a," a brash voice shouts. "Visit the gyp-sy for-tune-tell-er! See the fu-ture!"

You pass a wagon painted with a portrait of a beautiful fortuneteller. "Miss Teriosa," you read. She is covered in golden rings—dangling earrings in her ears and rows of bangles on her arms.

The crowd keeps forcing you along.

"Merry-go-round, merry-go-round!" shouts the brash voice. "Ride the carousel and reach for the ring! Win a prize!"

You can see the circus barker now, hard to miss in his costume of bright red and green. He is standing on a platform outside the main tent, holding a megaphone so large that his head disappears every time he calls into it.

"Step right up, ladies and gentlemen, and see the magic show!" he says. A little ballerina sets a small, red-draped table on the barker's platform. She is followed by a tall, slender gentleman in formal dress. The magician! He bows to the audience and plucks a bouquet of flowers from thin air. The crowd *ooohs*. Then he holds up a set of shining silver rings, one at a time. With a snap of his fingers, the rings are joined into a single clattering chain! The crowd *aaahs*.

"That's just a warm-up, folks," says the barker. "Magic show to your right. And don't forget the main attraction, the three-ring circus, right here in this tent! Yes, ladies and gents, we have lions and tigers, high-wire flyers and bareback riders, daredevils and dancing girls! Step right up to the Big Top! Three rings to see!"

Your head is spinning. It seems there are rings everywhere.

If you go to have your fortune told, turn to page 59.

If you want to ride the carousel, turn to page 45.

If you line up for the magic show, turn to page 72.

If you decide to enter the Big Top, turn to page 90.

from page 113

You decide to explore the Lost Lagoon. Climbing aboard the rowboat, you settle yourself on the rickety wooden seat. You survey the water carefully, but see no sign of snakes. The "crazy snake" may have been crazy, you think, but he didn't seem dangerous.

Using a weatherbeaten oar to push off from the shore, you glide across the silent lagoon, your back to the setting sun. The sun's final rays paint a shimmering path to the horizon.

The rhythmic squeaking of the oars makes you drowsy as you row. Your arms ache from the effort, but the horizon seems no closer. There is still only water as far as you can see.

You row on, waiting for nightfall. But even as the darkness spreads, the orange path of sunlight grows brighter. What's going on here? You study the setting sun. It has not set! It floats at the water's edge, a shining ball of light. Whatever you are rowing toward is *not* the sun.

You pull on the oars as hard as you can, and the clumsy little rowboat skims across the water. The horizon firms into a shoreline. The strange sun rises from the shore, opening onto the lagoon like an empty bowl. It is a grotto! And a light glows from within.

Deciding to drift, you rest your oars. But your boat somehow keeps moving. You peer over the side. You are being carried through the water by a carpet of swimming snakes!

"Wait! Stop!" you shout.

Paying no attention to you, the snakes moor your boat inside the grotto.

"Welcome to the Theater of Snakes," says a familiar voice. It is "Crazy Snake." "We're doing *A Thousand and One Arabian Nights*. Come, I'll show you." You follow him onto a stage and behind a painted backdrop.

"Our ballet troupe," he says proudly. At the back of the grotto, a line of snakes is rehearsing. Some clink tiny cymbals in their mouths as they dance and spin.

"These are our stars," says your guide, as you watch three snakes who practice a scene. Two are twined together, while the third speaks tragic lines at their feet.

"I wish I could stay for the performance," you say, "but I must be on my way."

"But you took our ferry boat," says the snake. "You must pay the fare."

You look back. The rowboat is gone, and there is no other way out of the grotto.

"What do you want?" you ask. "I have very little, but I will pay you what I can."

"We need a musician," says Crazy Snake, his fangs glinting. "And our little production runs for one thousand and one nights."

THE END

from page 119

It is growing dark, and you don't want to cause any further risk to your mysterious horse.

"I thank you for your offer to lead me to the hide-out of the Magician's Ring," you tell the robber-goblin, "but I shall meet with Mevar another time. There is something I must attend to first. Until we meet again!" You raise your cudgel in a salute to the bewildered bandit and gallop into the darkness.

Suddenly you find yourself riding on thin air. You pitch forward and roll to the ground. Someone sits next to you in the darkness.

"Whew, that was a close one!" she says. "I was afraid you were going to go with that horrible goblin."

"Who are you?" you ask. "You're not a prince!"

"I am the Princess Jian of Wandelmere," she answers, "and I thank you for your brave offer of help. I hope you were not hurt in your fall. But I wanted to get as far from the goblin as we could, so I galloped until I transformed. You must be tired. Shall I light a fire? I'd love an apple." She pauses thoughtfully. "Or do you think we have a chance of finding the goblin in the dark?"

It takes only a moment to get over your surprise. Then you answer.

If you want to make camp and rest for the night, turn to page 86.

If you want to try to sneak up on the goblin and follow him to Mevar's hide-out, turn to page 42.

from page 43

You decide to climb a tree to take stock of your surroundings. From your perch, you survey the tree-tops. The greenery stretches in every direction, but you can just make out a break in the trees far to the north. A clearing! It must be Mevar's hide-out.

You are halfway down the tree when you hear foot-steps on the path below you. Spotting two flashes of yellow in the mist, you flatten yourself along a branch.

Soon the robber-goblin strides into view, accompanied by an ogre.

"It was right about here," says the goblin. "She was sleeping just as pretty as you please, so I carried her off to the hide-out. And guess who she turns out to be? Princess Jian of Wandelmere! This morning she's a horse once more. Ho, ho!"

"Too bad you couldn't carry them both," says the ogre. "Mevar will be mad as a magpie if the other gets away."

"He couldn't have gone far," says the goblin. "And he's sure to stay on the path. Let's keep going."

You wait for them to vanish from sight. Then, leaving the path behind, you strike out into the forest, heading north, your cudgel on your shoulder. When you think you may have lost your way, you climb another tree to check your bearings.

On and on you walk, as darkness slowly falls again. You *must* find the Magician's hide-out!

Turn to page 99.

30

"The fewer enemies the better," says Jian. "Let's find a hiding place quickly."

Scanning the area, you spot a leafy oak. "I think we should climb that tree on the other side of the clearing," you say. "The one near the treasure. But first I have a plan!"

You creep back to the wooden cage and cut through the ropes that bind the sapling bars. The cage sways and creaks, but does not collapse. You return to Jian and head toward the oak tree, keeping to the outskirts of the clearing.

"Hurry," you whisper. "The cage is balanced for now, but the first strong gust of wind will knock it over. The crash should bring them running!"

You sneak behind a grumbling group of ogres and dwarfs, and climb to safety in the limbs of the oak. Stretching out on a branch, you peer below. A screen of softly rustling leaves shields you from sight, but you can easily make out the glowing campfires and the pile of treasure that sparkles in the firelight.

Suddenly you hear a twig snap in the forest. Footsteps! Moments later, a powerful voice echoes through the clearing.

"Who guards the Ring?" it booms.

Every goblin and ogre and dwarf stands at attention. And their thirty voices reply in unison: *"We are the Ring who guard the Ring!"*

"And who is the Master of the Ring?" bellows the voice.

"*Mevar! Mevar! Mevar!*" they chant.

This oath of allegiance done, a figure strides directly beneath your oak tree and stops near the heap of treasure.

"It is Mevar," whispers Jian.

The Magician is not dressed for forest life. He wears a top hat and tails, and an elegant opera cloak lined with scarlet satin is slung across one shoulder. Despite his finery, Mevar is a fright to behold. His cruel face is made up in bright, flat colors, like that of a scowling scarecrow or a twisted demon doll. And his hair sticks up from his head like porcupine quills.

The robber-goblin marches forward to report to Mevar. You overhear the words "Princess" and "Wandelmere," but a rising wind rustles the leaves around you too loudly for you to make out the rest. You hear a *crash*, however, as the wind brings down the wooden cage.

All is confusion in the firelit clearing. Pounding feet run to and fro, and anxious voices cry, "They've escaped!" "After them!" "To the forest!" You catch sight of the robber-goblin, who backs slowly away from Mevar, frantically explaining and waving his hands.

"Find them, you fools!" Mevar commands. His ring-members scatter in every direction.

Mevar glares at the simpering goblin. "I should turn you into a worm!" he barks. Then his tone changes, and he puts a reassuring arm around the goblin's shoulders. "But you did well to bring them to me. They'll be captured soon enough. And then I'll turn them into something *really* amusing. Ah, ha, ha! Or maybe I'll just keep them here, as pets!"

"Here?" asks the goblin doubtfully.

"Worried about the Ring are you?" says Mevar. "Have no fear. How could they guess that of all the rings in this towering mountain of jewels and gold, it's a plain iron ring that gives me my power! Now, be off, and join the search!"

The goblin hurries into the forest, and Mevar leans against the heap of treasure below you, patiently waiting.

At last you are alone in the clearing with Mevar the Magician. You know you must act fast, before his guards return, and before he can reach for his magic ring. You motion for Jian to remain silent, and quietly pull the heavy block of ringwood from your rucksack. Taking careful aim, you hurl the wood with all your might. It conks Mevar squarely on the head, and the Magician slumps to the ground.

You scramble down the oak, Jian right behind you.

"Run to the treasure heap and look for an iron ring," you tell her. "You can burn the ringwood figures as you search. I'll be there to help in a moment."

You cross the clearing to the fallen cage and find several long ropes. Returning to the unconscious Mevar, you bind him securely to the oak. Then you hurry to help Princess Jian.

She is buried to her ankles in cast-off diamonds, pearls, and gold, digging her way through the mountain of treasure. She throws a ruby necklace over her shoulder and dumps a bag of silver coins at your feet. "We *must* find the iron ring to break the spell," she says. "See? The ringwood will not burn!"

You look at a nearby campfire, which burns brightly around a pile of ringwood carvings. But the carvings might just as well be made of stone, for they do not burn.

Diving into the treasure heap, you scatter gems in every direction. You empty golden cups, ivory boxes, ebony cases; you find emerald rings, sapphire rings, platinum and moonstone rings. Nowhere do you find an iron ring.

"We just have to find the ring!" Jian moans. "It's almost dawn!"

"Mevar is beginning to stir," you warn, "and the guards will return when they give up hope of finding us!"

Only a huge wooden treasure chest remains to be searched. You strain to open the heavy lid. Inside is a curious chess set carved of ringwood. The pieces are all forest creatures—goblins, giants, ogres, and elves.

"The Ring of Thieves must be enchanted, too!" says Jian. "But where is the iron ring?"

"Ah, ha, ha!" cries a voice. "You'll never find it!" Mevar is awake.

"Guards!" he yells, struggling to get free of the ropes. Two husky dwarfs run into the clearing.

Suddenly you see it! Fastened to the chest is a ringwood handle in the shape of a dragon. And clasped in the dragon's teeth hangs a heavy iron ring.

"Stop!" you cry to the dwarfs, as you pull the ring from the chest.

"Stop!" shrieks Mevar.

"I command that Mevar's spells be broken!" you say, holding the ring up before you.

The ringwood carvings burst into flame. Jian adds the chess set to the blazing bonfire, and the clearing begins to fill with the members of the Magician's Ring. But the giant is shy, and the gnomes are sweet; the elves are merry, and the dwarfs are friendly. The goblin runs forward to give you a grateful hug.

Gripping the ring, you utter one last command. "Change Mevar into a good-hearted man! And let all those present forget about the powers of this Ring!"

Suddenly Mevar is no more, and in his place is a gallant prince. You untie him from the tree.

"Thank you for freeing me, Minstrel," says the prince. "You shall have as much of my treasure as you can carry!"

THE END

from page 9

The horse gives you a pleading look. He stamps a foreleg on the ground with impatience and shakes his mane.

The crone may know a secret, but perhaps the horse knows something as well. You waste no further time, and spring onto the horse's back.

"You'll regret this, fool!" the crone croaks as you gallop away.

The horse has no saddle, and you cling to his neck as he races through the cobbled streets of the town. He does not stop until you reach a shabby barn on the outskirts of Wandelmere.

You dismount. The horse trots inside the cool, dank barn and leads you to a haystack in a corner. He begins to scatter the hay with one hoof, until you laugh with understanding. He has uncovered a pile of nuts and apples, carefully buried in the hay.

"Did you hide this here?" you ask. The horse nods his head yes. You busily dig out the rest of the food as the horse chews with distaste on a mouthful of hay. You remove your cloak from your rucksack and pack up the food. Then you spread the cloak over the horse's broad back.

"You are a royal horse indeed," you comment. The horse agrees again. "Are you a prince?" you ask. The horse will not answer. "Do you know where to look for Mevar the Magician?" The horse slowly shakes his head no.

You try to hide your disappointment. "Well, let's be off, and we shall ask along the way," you say cheerfully, and you climb on his back once more.

You sing and tell tales to the horse as you ride northward. Soon the Kingdom of Wandelmere is far behind you, and you venture into country you have never traveled before.

You come to a thick forest. A narrow path leads through a grove of towering pines, and you follow it into the forest. The trees block out the sun.

It is late afternoon and you are tired, so you begin to search for a place to camp. The horse shudders and you shiver in the sudden coolness. A feeling of danger creeps up your spine. You pull the cowled neck of your tunic over your head like a hood. The front of the collar covers your nose and chin.

You see a flash of yellow in a thicket ahead of you. Then it is gone. The horse quivers and pricks up his ears, and walks slowly toward the thicket. You pause to pick up a hefty branch from the ground, to use as a cudgel if need be.

"You there!" you call toward the thicket in your most commanding voice. "Show yourself! But I warn you, I am armed!"

"Are you now?" answers a calm voice at your back. "Why, so am I."

You quickly twist around to see a ruthless-looking goblin standing behind you on the path. He wears the garb of a forest bandit, with a bright yellow kerchief at his throat. He is aiming an arrow at your heart.

The forest is thick on both sides of the path, and there is nowhere to run. You know it will soon be dark. You would like to get rid of this troublesome goblin before your horse turns into a person.

If you attack the goblin with your cudgel, turn to page 81.

If you wait to see what he wants, turn to page 118.

You decide to try to silence the bells in the Tower of Mevar. Perhaps the note one of them sounds is the mysterious Magician's Ring.

The tower is unguarded, and appears to be deserted. The ground floor contains only a sweeping stone staircase that circles upward.

From where you stand at the entrance, the clamorous bell song seems dull and far away. But you can feel vibrations in the wooden banister as you climb the stairs.

Once again you are grateful for your unusual strength. You climb and climb the windowless staircase, judging your position only by the increasing volume of the bells. Even with dough in your ears, they are painfully loud. You wish they would *stop*.

Finally you reach the top of the staircase. Pushing open a wooden door, you are forced to cover your ears, the noise is so deafening.

The tower is not deserted! A wizened old bell ringer occupies the tower, his ears muffled in rags. He is surrounded by a jungle of bell ropes. Up and down he jumps as he sets the bell clappers clanging.

You tap his shoulder as he hops onto a bell rope.

"Stop ringing!" you shout into his bandaged ear, but he does not understand.

"Ring, ring!" he cackles, hauling on another rope.

You will have to stop the bells yourself. Grabbing a swinging bell rope, you tug as hard as you can to still the clapper. But the rope seems to have a life of its own, and it pulls you off your feet.

As you swing through the air, you feel an overwhelming urge to ring the next bell. And the next! To hear them all ringing at once! That would be glorious.

"Free at last!" shouts the mad bell ringer. "Free after thirty years!" He casts his earmuffs to the floor in triumph and scampers down the stairs, as spry as a colt.

You know your duty. You will ring the bells of Ringdell until someone comes to take your place.

THE END

from page 28

The goblin can lead you instantly to the Magician's Ring, and you hate to let the chance slip by.

"Let's trail the goblin," you reply to Princess Jian.

"But even if we can find him again in the darkness," says Jian, "he might see us first. This forest is his home, and he knows it well. He could be watching us right now. And what if we meet more of Mevar's men?"

"We must be careful and silent," you answer. "Let's try to follow the goblin to the secret meeting place of the Magician's Ring. We might never find it by ourselves."

You stand, and help Jian to her feet. She wraps your cloak around her shoulders. You can see little more of her than the two sparks of light in her eyes.

You set off again, back the way you came. You stumble blindly together in the darkness as you feel your way along the narrow path, trying to move as quietly as deer. You squint into the darkness, hoping to catch a glimpse of a yellow kerchief or the flash of a golden ring. You trip over roots and bump into branches. Solid shapes dissolve into murky shadows, and shadows turn out to be trees. The spooky silence is interrupted by crackles and rustles, howls and hoots.

Many hours pass, but you see no one. And you do not emerge from the wood.

"We are lost," whispers Jian.

"Completely lost," you agree.

"Let's rest here and have something to eat," Jian suggests.

You sink wearily to the ground. You rummage through your sack and find two apples. Jian's hand reaches for one in the darkness. You bite into the other apple with a thirsty crunch, and finish it off in a trice. Suddenly you are overcome by a delicious drowsiness. Your eyelids feel heavy and your head swims with sleepiness.

You awaken to a drizzling rain. The day is gray and chilly. Next to you lie your cudgel, your damp cloak, and two apple cores. Jian has vanished.

You stretch stiffly, and your stomach rumbles with hunger. You wrap yourself in your cloak. Then you search the ground for footprints. You are on a woodland path, but the rain has turned the earth to mud. The only track you find fits one of your own boots.

You are alone, confused, and hopelessly lost.

If you follow your own tracks back the way you came, turn to page 56.

If you continue in the direction you were going, turn to page 109.

If you climb a tree to try to get your bearings, turn to page 29.

44

You don't want to take any chances on enchantment.

"No, thank you," you tell the witch. "I've already had my supper."

"Then off you go with no further help from me!" snaps the witch. "If you take no chances, you'll never be a match for Mevar the Magician!"

The door of the cottage swings open and you are left on your own once more.

Turn to page 22.

You decide to try the carousel. The ride is in a bright striped tent, filled with jingling music.

You watch the riders pass by in a whirl as the merry-go-round turns. A wooden hand moves in and out of the curious box at one side of the tent. The hand holds forth a shiny brass ring. Perhaps it is the key to Mevar's power!

The riders squeal with delight as the circling carousel brings them just within reach of the ring. Up and down they go. But no one is skillful enough to snatch the ring.

The music slows and the ride comes to an end. Men, women, and children clamber down from the wooden animals, and a new crowd scrambles up for their turn.

"Ride the merry-go-round and reach for the ring!" calls the barker. Climbing onto the ride, you study the wooden animals. There are ponies, of course, and lions, an ostrich, zebras, and a giraffe. You select the ostrich. It has a long neck you can hold on to as you reach for the ring.

The music begins and the carousel starts to turn. The carousel gains speed, and the fairground circles by in a blur.

Up goes the ostrich as you near the ring. But as you pass it, the ostrich sinks down again, and the hand pulls the ring beyond your reach. Around and around you ride. All too soon the music slows and the ride ends. The merry-go-round empties and people hurry off to the Big Top. New riders take their places.

Ready for a second try, you switch to an orange pony. The carousel starts up once more. This time you brush the shining ring with the tips of your fingers, but you can't get a hold on it.

Several tries later, you choose the giraffe. The fairground is getting dark and the crowd is thinning. There are only a dozen riders on the carousel. You are a little dizzy by now and almost fall as you strain to reach the ring.

You try a zebra, a purple pony, and a lion. Several times you touch the ring, and once you almost get your fingers hooked around it, but you always spin away before you can get a firm grip.

Finally you are the only rider left on the carousel. The world is spinning and you feel as if you are moving up and down, even when you are standing still.

"How long are you going to ride this thing?" asks the barker.

"Until I reach the ring," you answer.

"Suit yourself," says the barker with an evil grin. "But I'm finished for the night." He starts the ride up once more and disappears through a flap in the tent.

The carousel is moving too quickly to jump off, and no matter how far you stretch, the ring stays forever beyond your grasp.

Around and around and around you go.

THE END

48

from page 80

You set on your way once again, leaving the noisy valley of Ringdell behind you. You have decided to search for the dragon's lair.

A rough path leads from the valley to a mountainous region studded with rocks. Remembering that dragons breathe flames and often inhabit caves, you search the landscape for signs of fire or openings in the rock. Your reasoning is soon rewarded. You find an ashy trail that leads to a gap in the side of a gloomy cliff.

Cautiously peering into the gap, you see a long, narrow corridor running deep into the mountainside. It is lit by torches and is just a dragon's-breadth wide. From the depths of the cave comes a high-pitched wailing roar, the like of which you have never heard before.

You enter the gap and creep along a torchlit corridor. The passage appears to end abruptly at a wall of jagged rock. As you approach, however, you see that the corridor veers sharply to the left.

You follow the torches through countless twists and descending turns, tunneling far into the mountain. You pass through a hollow cavern, dripping tunnels, and passageways piled with rocky rubble. Suddenly a cave opens before you, filled with stalactites and stalagmites like the teeth inside a dragon's mouth.

Again you hear the wailing sound. It is as terrifying as a monster's roar, but as heartrending as a baby's cry. And it is much louder.

You examine the cave. There is an orange light glowing from an area bare of stalagmites at the center of the floor. You dislodge a torch from the wall and make your way through the maze of stalactites and stalagmites until you reach the orange glow. You see a hole in the floor that opens to a circular pit below.

The opening is rimmed by stalagmites, spindly and huge. They form a circular balcony of fanglike growths, like a row of pointy teeth, overlooking the pit. Sheltered behind a sturdy stalagmite, you have a clear view of the lower cave. You douse your torch. *There it is!*

Near one wall of the pit you see a large golden ring, the height of a man, magically suspended in midair. The ring hangs before an alcove cut into the wall of the pit. In the alcove is an empty throne. And chained to the wall opposite the throne is a baby dragon, wailing pitifully. Small puffs of smoke rise from his nostrils, and a cloudy tear drops from his eye to sizzle like acid on the cave floor. You are nervously wondering if his mother is nearby when you hear a voice echo across the cave.

"Oh, stop your bellyaching," says the voice, "or I'll send you to the mines with your mother. Some guard-dragon you are. You're about as fierce as an elf!"

A grumbling figure emerges from behind a stalag-mite and climbs down a silken rope ladder into the pit. He is uglier than anyone you have ever seen. The dragon sniffles and strains at his chain.

"Behave yourself!" commands the hideous figure. "Mevar the Great has no time for your nonsense. My powers weaken and I must use my Ring. I have work to do!"

You watch as the Magician steps through the golden ring. The ring glows for a moment with a greenish light, then fades once again. Mevar sits on the throne in the alcove and takes a deep breath. Before your eyes he transforms into a handsome prince!

A satisfied grin crosses his face as he climbs back onto the ladder. "I have a princess to enchant!" he gloats. "Now guard my Ring well!" He passes behind a stalagmite and disappears.

This is your chance to destroy the Magician's Ring! But how will you do it? You are not sure you want to climb into a pit with a dragon, even if he is a baby. But the dragon's chain seems secure. Perhaps if you pass through the Ring yourself, you will have enough strength to break it. But what if the Ring has another effect?

You think of the rhyme you heard in Ringdell.

How *did* that verse go? *"You will find it if you choose, the kind of ring a baby chews."* A teething ring! No wonder the baby dragon is wailing so—he must be cutting teeth!

If you want to think of a way to destroy the Ring from where you are, turn to page 58.

If you want to climb into the pit, turn to page 13.

from page 83

You decide the horse's whinny was a signal—maybe a call for help. You gingerly press your shoulder. It is less sore already, and the arrow has left only a scratch. Picking up your fallen cudgel, you hurry in the direction of the horse's cry.

There it is again—a loud whinny!

You creep through the underbrush and part the branches of a dense, leafy bush.

The goblin is pulling at the rope he cast around the horse's neck. "Come on, horsey," he pleads. But the horse stands fast.

Suddenly, the horse is gone. In his place stands a lovely auburn-haired woman!

"Ho! And who may you be?" asks the surprised bandit. "A fugitive from Wandelmere? Won't Mevar be pleased!"

"I am the Princess Jian of Wandelmere," answers the woman, "and I command you to release me at once!"

"Mevar rules here, my lady," says the robber-goblin, "and off we go to meet him. Ho, ho!"

The goblin tightens the rope around Princess Jian's neck, and pulls her after him into the dense wood. They are soon swallowed by the dark forest. You will have to hurry to catch up to them.

Turn to page 99.

from page 88

Rising to your feet, you creep toward the sleeping unicorn. She is breathing deeply and does not stir.

You reach for the golden ring encircling her horn. As your fingers grasp the cool metal, her eyelids flutter open. Reflected in her eye you see your own guilty face. She makes no sound. But a cry echoes in your mind. "Betrayer!"

You feel a blinding whiteness in your throat and you know you have been touched by the unicorn's horn.

You wake up in an empty clearing wreathed in mist. Around your neck is a golden collar. You can no longer speak or sing.

THE END

You decide to find out what the crone can tell you about the Magician's Ring. Besides, you have been traveling all day and singing all night, and you are exhausted.

You wander into a deserted house, choose an empty bed, and fall asleep.

Awakening refreshed at dusk, you walk briskly through the narrow streets and alleys of the town until you reach a run-down cottage just beyond the walls of Wandelmere. A thin column of smoke rises from its crumbling chimney, and from inside you can hear the crone humming and cackling to herself.

"Come in, Minstrel," she calls as you approach. You push open the door and enter the cottage. Its simple furnishings are warmly lit by a fire on a stone hearth, over which the crone is tending a huge, cast-iron cooking pot.

"Sit down, sit down, Minstrel," says the crone as she stirs the bubbling cauldron. You move toward a rustic table and chairs, but you stay on your feet.

"Who are you?" you ask. "And what can you tell me of the Magician's Ring?"

"My, my, you're an anxious one," the crone remarks. "I wouldn't be in such a hurry to meet up with Mevar if I were you! Eh, eh! Not on an empty stomach, especially." She samples a spoonful of murky liquid from the cauldron and smacks her lips. "You'll stay for my soup, won't you? Mushrooms and rare herbs. It's a specialty of the house! Won't you dine with the Witch of Wandelmere?"

A witch! You eye the concoction suspiciously. It smells peculiar, but not unpleasant.

You are hungry, and have no wish to offend a witch by refusing her cooking. You want her to tell you of Mevar and his Ring. But what if the soup is really a witch's brew?

If you accept the witch's soup, turn to page 120.

If you politely refuse the witch's invitation to supper, turn to page 44.

56

from page 43

You decide to retrace your steps. Perhaps you will find a clue to the whereabouts of Jian, or discover the route to Mevar's hide-out.

You drape your cloak around you and set off once again. The rain has stopped, but morning mist still blankets the ground. In some spots it is so thick you can hardly see your feet.

On and on you walk until, exhausted, you squat at the base of a tree to rest. Your toe hits something on the ground. It is a pair of apple cores, shriveled and brown. You are back where you started from. Your heart sinks. It is past midday, and you are as lost as ever.

Your heart lifts again as you hear hoofbeats on the path. Your face lights with a welcoming smile as Jian, a horse once more, trots into view.

But your smile fades quickly. For through her nose is a golden ring. And on her back rides the robber-goblin.

"Lost your horsey?" jeers the goblin. "Some highwayman you'd make! A disgrace to the trade, you are. I'll take you to Mevar, all right, but not as one of us!"

You look behind you, ready to run, but a muscular dwarf stands on one side of you and a tough-looking gnome guards the other. Both wear single gold earrings and sport yellow kerchiefs at their throats. One whips a blindfold around your eyes, while the other binds your hands. You are led roughly through the forest, then thrown into a pit.

You hear a whinny above your head, and the voice of the robber-goblin.

"Imagine him believing you're a princess, eh, Mevara? Ho, ho! It's a good thing your brother left you to look after Wandelmere. Mevar's a shrewd one, all right! You'd better get back now, in case any more do-gooders wander along. Ho, ho, ho!"

You hear a neighing laugh in reply, and a soft thudding of hoofbeats, which soon fades away.

Darkness falls. Wishing you had heeded the warning of the crone of Wandelmere, you wonder how you will escape from the deep forest pit.

THE END

from page 50

You show yourself at the edge of the pit. As you look into the dragon's mouth, he roars feebly. Sure enough, his gums are red and swollen, and you can see the beginnings of his pointy teeth. The rocky floor around him is pitted with holes from his burning teardrops.

"Dragon!" you call. "Is that *your* ring?" He moans tearfully and nods in reply.

"If you want to get loose, you must cry onto your chain," you say.

The dragon looks doubtful, but does as he is told. Soon the metal links begin to sizzle!

"Concentrate on a single link," you say. It works. The massive chain snaps!

The dragon bounds happily to the golden ring and grips it in his budding teeth. The ring begins to glow green, and the baby dragon begins to grow!

You back away slowly. Suddenly, with an explosive flash of bright green light, the ring breaks in two. The dragon's tears have eaten their way through the precious gold, and you are alone in the cave with a young dragon, who continues to chew on his favorite toy.

You retrace your steps through the tunnels. In the first cavern, you pass a hideous prince, bawling loudly and pounding his fists on the rock.

You come out into the light of day. The bells of Ringdell are silent, and you know that all will be well in Wandelmere.

THE END

from page 24 / from page 75

You make your way to the fortuneteller's wagon to consult Miss Teriosa. A beaded curtain of colored glass hangs across the doorway, concealing the dark interior. Two young ladies leave the wagon, giggling excitedly, and hurry off into the crowd.

Long, slender hands, aglitter with rings, part the clattering curtain, and Miss Teriosa appears. Her arms and ankles, ears and toes, are adorned with golden rings. She wears a ruffled skirt of many colors, a bright embroidered shawl, and a wreath of red flowers in her dark curls. She is as beautiful as her portrait. And you can see from her strange, unfocused gaze that she is blind.

"Seeker of the future," she says to you, "enter and be seated." She beckons with a ring-laden finger and disappears through the rattling curtain.

You follow her into the wagon. In the dim light you can make out a table and chairs. Miss Teriosa gestures to an empty chair and seats herself opposite you.

"Hush," she says, holding a finger to her lips. "Give me your palms." For several minutes she silently traces the lines on the palms of your hands. The strings of glass beads click softly and glitter like prisms in the doorway. Finally she speaks.

"You may ask me three questions. I speak only the truth."

"Do you have the Magician's Ring?" you ask. "The Ring of Mevar?" Miss Teriosa shows no surprise at your first question, but slowly shakes her head.

"I do not have the ring you seek," she answers.

You wait for her to say more, but she has fallen silent once again. You ask your second question.

"Where is Mevar the Magician to be found?"

"Beneath the tent," replies the fortuneteller. "I can see no more."

"What can you tell me of the Magician's Ring?" you ask.

"I have never seen it," answers Miss Teriosa. "I know only that it jingles like music. You must find the jingling sound."

Your three questions are up. Miss Teriosa releases your hands and turns away from you. You do not think she is Mevar.

Exiting through the sparkling curtain into the light, you search the fairground for unusual tents and strain your ears for a jingling noise.

A cheerful jingling music comes from a tent to your left that shelters the carousel. And farther on is a giant tent, the canopy called the Big Top.

If you want to ride the carousel, turn to page 45.

If you investigate the Big Top, turn to page 90.

62

from page 121

Choosing the village as your destination, you aim toward the tower that spirals up in the distance. You descend into the valley and set off through the colorful meadows. The sweet smell of wildflowers fills your head with summery thoughts. But your enjoyment is soon banished by the din of the bells, clanging louder and louder as you near the village.

Clapping your hands over your ears, you enter the town. You are not surprised that few villagers are about. You duck into the first open shop you come to, a bakery.

"Hello there!" says the baker, a jolly round fellow. "Come in for a bit of dough, have you?"

"Dough?" You are puzzled. You introduce yourself and ask where you are.

"Why, you're in Ringdell," answers the baker. "I'm afraid there's not much call for a minstrel here. It's the bells, you see, in the Tower of Mevar. Enchanted. Ring, ring, ring. That's what the dough is for. It makes the best earplugs in town!"

You remember the witch's words: *not a finger ring*...Could the enchanted ringing of the bells be the Magician's Ring?

Pushing some dough into your ears, you thank the baker and hurry out to the street. Perhaps you should try to stop the bells.

Making your way toward the tower, you come upon a group of children. They are holding hands and dancing in a circle. You see that their mouths are moving and realize that they are singing a song.

You pull a plug of dough from one ear and pause to listen. The tower looms nearby.

"Ring-around-the-rosy," the children sing, the bells almost drowning out their words. Another ring!

If you stay to listen to the children's game, turn to page 80.

If you want to try to stop the bells, turn to page 39.

from page 83

You decide to stay where you are, in case the horse should return. Your shoulder still pains you, and you are bruised from your fall. Removing the goblin's arrow from your rucksack, you lean against the sack to rest. The trees of the forest rustle softly.

Gradually, the rustling grows louder. Something is coming your way—and it doesn't sound like a horse. You grip the arrow like a spear and grope for your cudgel in the shadows.

"Some help you are!" says a weary voice at the edge of the forest.

Peering across the path, you see a young woman emerge from a thick hedge, dragging behind her the unconscious form of the robber-goblin. She shakes her dark-red hair from her eyes as she drops the goblin at your feet.

"Wh-who are you?" you ask.

The woman tears a strip from the hem of her gown and begins to bandage your shoulder.

"I am Princess Jian of Wandelmere," she replies. "This goblin took me to the hiding place of the Magician's Ring. I tried to escape into the forest, but he chased me! Then I knocked him out with a hoof—didn't you hear me signal for help? You must guard him closely now, so he cannot warn Mevar."

You watch in amazement as the Princess pulls the goblin's shirt and trousers over her own delicate gown.

"But what are you doing, Your Highness?" you ask. "Don't you want me to come with you?"

"I'm disguising myself as a bandit," she answers, "to infiltrate the Magician's Ring. And this is something I must do, myself, for the people of Wandelmere. I appreciate your bravery, Minstrel, and your generous offer of help. But you are already wounded, and you might have gotten us killed. I'll continue on my own. Good-bye!"

The Princess ties the yellow kerchief around her neck and disappears into the forest.

You are left alone to guard the goblin, who looks much less fierce in his underwear. It is up to you to make sure he doesn't get away. You hope the Princess remembers to come back for you after she finds the Magician's Ring!

THE END

You cautiously approach the door to the ringmaster's wagon. You can hear objects bouncing off the walls and crashing to the floor inside. The ringmaster is having a tantrum!

"Curse him!" he cries. "Ever since that Tamerlane came to my circus, he thinks he runs the show. My performers quit or disappear, we keep getting more and more animal acts, the animals are crazy...."

You do not wait to hear any more. Tamerlane must be Mevar!

To find the animal trainer, turn to page 114.

You decide to take a chance and accompany the goblin to Mevar's hiding place.

"I would be honored to meet your master," you say. "Let's be off."

Your horse shakes his head and stamps his hooves in dismay, but you pat his neck reassuringly. "We might never find Mevar on our own," you whisper into his ear. "Let's go."

"This way then," winks the goblin. He strides to the thicket and lifts a twisted clump of branches. It opens like a flap. You can see that the thicket behind it has been hollowed to form a tunnel through the brambles and leaves. It is just large enough for the horse to get through if he lowers his head.

You dismount and hold the flap aside for the horse. Then you, too, follow the goblin into the leafy tunnel.

Inside it is quite dark, but you have to walk only a short way before the tunnel widens, and the growth overhead thins to reveal an evening sky and a rising moon. You walk ahead with the goblin while the horse follows.

You begin to hear the rumble of many voices, and you smell roasting game. Emerging from the tunnel, you come to an abrupt halt.

You are in a large clearing dotted with campfires. Shadowy groups of figures are gathered around each fire, laughing and drinking brew. You could never have imagined such a collection of scoundrels. Gruesome

gnomes guffaw at a goblin's tale of treachery; evil elves snicker as they pick the pockets of a snoring giant; dangerous dwarfs sharpen daggers on their teeth. There are about thirty villains in all, and each one is shadier than the next.

Every member of this ring of thieves wears a band of gold—here on a finger, there through an ear or a nose.

At the center of the clearing a huge heap of treasure glitters in the firelight. You see ropes of emeralds and strands of pearls, crystal cups and jewel-filled coffers, swords and statues, crowns and thrones.

"Ah-roo!" shouts the robber-goblin. "I've brought a highwayman to meet the Master." All eyes turn your way. The goblin ushers you and your horse to a crackling campfire.

"He don't look like no highwayman to me," growls a bearlike bully. "Who'd you rob today?" he demands.

"I rode into Wandelmere," you answer, "but the place was full of animals!"

At this they all laugh long and loudly.

"One of Mevar's best!" snorts a pirate.

"Now he goes about as pretty as you please while Wandelmere's a farmyard!" hoots a hawk-eyed crook.

"Where is this Mevar?" you ask. Your horse stirs nervously and takes a few steps back toward the wood.

The goblin replies. "He is often gone for days at a time. He'll be back in a night or two. Come, eat and drink, and tell us who you've robbed or kidnapped."

Suddenly thirty pairs of beady eyes are peering beyond you with suspicion. You turn to see your horse fading away. In his place appears a richly dressed princess with long auburn hair and eyes wide with fright. She still wears your cloak.

"Intruders from Wandelmere! Grab them!" shouts a gnome. Strong hands pin both of your arms to your sides. Your cudgel drops to the ground. The Princess tries to flee into the wood, but she is quickly captured. You are both dragged to a small wooden cage in a corner of the clearing and penned inside.

You immediately invent a story and hope you can free the Princess later. "Wait!" you cry. "Let me go! I stole that horse from Wandelmere! I didn't know it was a spy!"

"Save your stories for Mevar," says an ogre. "Your trick has not worked."

You question your companion. "Who are you, anyway?"

"I am Princess Jian of Wandelmere," she whispers. "I did not mean to mislead you, but I was afraid you would refuse to take me with you if you knew my true identity. My father forbade me to leave the castle. But I felt I had to try to help my people."

"We'll find a way out of this," you assure her. "And then we'll find Mevar and his Magician's Ring." But you have your doubts.

You examine the cage. The bars are stout saplings lashed together with thick twine. The floor and ceiling are wooden planks. The door is padlocked.

You still have your rucksack. You are certain you could saw through the wooden bars with your carving knife, but nine sharp-eyed gnomes are guarding you from a nearby campfire.

"You know," says Princess Jian, "I can easily break this small cage apart in the morning when I transform into a horse again. Let's just eavesdrop for a while. Perhaps we'll learn more of this Ring."

"That's a good idea," you agree. "But what if Mevar comes back? Perhaps I could lull them all to sleep with my lute. I know lullabies that will soothe raging beasts. Then we could escape. Or we could steal all of the rings we find and hope one is the Magician's Ring."

"But how will we know?" says Jian.

You both think.

If you decide to eavesdrop, turn to page 14.

If you decide to sing lullabies, turn to page 104.

from page 24

Joining the crowd lined up for the magic show, you file through a canvas flap into a darkened tent. Inside, you notice a small doorway to one side of the stage. While the audience scurries to fill the benches, you slip through the door.

You find yourself backstage in a room filled with props. There are huge wooden boxes, trunks overflowing with sequined costumes, a ventriloquist's dummy, silk flowers, and a cage of white rabbits.

You do not see the linking rings the magician used outside. But you do spot a tall, paneled cabinet. Sliding open the cabinet door, you are disappointed to find it empty, even of shelves.

"Hurry, Esmeralda, it's showtime!" says a deep voice. You hear footsteps, and a girl answers, "I'm coming!" It's the magician and the ballerina!

You duck into the cabinet and close the door. There is room for you to stand up inside, and light filters through thin diagonal slits in the panels.

You hear a burst of applause as the magician and his assistant make their entrances onto the stage. But backstage you still hear heavy footsteps.

Sliding open the cabinet door a crack, you see two burly stagehands dressed in black from head to toe. They are preparing the props for the magic show. Outside, the crowd ooohs and aaahs. You shut the cabinet door.

"Bring that next," you hear the ballerina instruct. "And don't forget the swords!"

Suddenly the cabinet is moving!

"This thing's heavy," says one of the stagehands. The other grunts in agreement. "Push it right under the spotlight," he says.

They push you onto the stage! The audience cheers, and bright light spills through the slits in the wood.

"For my next illusion," says the magician, "I shall perform the death-defying Sorcery of the Swords. Observe, an ordinary cabinet." You hear the ring of steel as a gleaming sword is suddenly thrust through the cabinet, narrowly missing your nose! The audience murmurs.

You crouch at the bottom of the cabinet, hoping you can find a way out before the magician opens the cabinet door to the audience—or before he skewers you! Another sword zings through the cabinet just above your head.

You desperately run your hand across the floor of the cabinet. Perhaps there is a false bottom. Your fingers touch a small button, and you press. The tip of a sword just misses you as the floor of the cabinet springs open and you fall into a cramped crawlspace.

The magician announces, "I will now open the cabinet." You close the false bottom of the contraption just in time.

"As you can see, it is quite empty, and the swords penetrate clear through," continues the magician. "My lovely assistant will now enter the cabinet," says the magician. You decide you'd better move before Esmeralda lands on your head!

Beneath the stage, you find a trap door, which leads you back to the prop room. Out front, the audience gasps and applauds loudly.

Many of the props have been shifted around, and you spot the set of silver rings on a small table. They are still interlocked in a chain, and you shake them to see if they will come apart. You hear a deep laugh. The magician is standing behind you!

"Ho, ho, not like that!" he says. "Here, I'll show you." He makes a slight motion and the rings clink onto his arm, one at a time. "Amateur magician, are you?" He winks knowingly. Snap! The rings form a chain again. "Why don't you take these and practice?" says the magician, handing you the rings. "I've got a dozen sets. But you're not supposed to be backstage. You'll have to leave now."

"Th-thank you," you tell the magician, backing out of the tent.

He couldn't be Mevar. This magician's tricks are only circus illusions. The rings are made of common metal.

You will have to search elsewhere.

If you want to ride the carousel, turn to page 45.

If you head for the Big Top, turn to page 90.

If you decide to have your fortune told, turn to page 59.

76

from page 97 / from page 108

You decide to search the earth for the Magician's Ring. Mevar, you think, could not use a ring as far away as the moon and stars.

You slide the lever until the gigantic telescope swings downward to focus on the earth. The telescope is so powerful you can see the veins in every leaf on every tree, each tiny ant, and every ant's antennae. Things are so magnified you can hardly tell what you are looking at. Grains of sand look like a stone wall, while a tropical forest turns out to be a field of green grass. How can you hope to find the Ring with so much to see?

Giving the telescope a final spin, you decide to trust your luck.

"Dr. Moonami!" you call, ready to take your leave.

"What? Found something already? Well, let's have a look," says the astrologer, clambering up the ladder.

"No, I just want..."

"Oh, you want your chart, do you? Want to know the future? Well, you'll have to wait. It can take a year, maybe two, to cast a good chart. Now, let's see what you've found. Mmm hmm." The astrologer makes several adjustments to the telescope. "Ah ha! Yes, yes, that could be what you're looking for, all right. Could be..."

You peer through the eyepiece once again. A rippling band of color passes before your eyes. After a moment, you realize you are looking at a snake! He is rolling along a woodland path with his tail in his mouth, upright like a child's hoop. Or a ring!

"If you want to follow him, the snake is on the path behind my observatory," says Dr. Moonami. "But of course you'll want to wait for your chart!"

If you decide to see where the snake is rolling, turn to page 112.

If you'd rather resume your journey in another direction, turn to page 87.

Or you can wait a year or two for your chart to be finished!

from page 17

You decide to sing the bandits to sleep with your powerful lullabies. Making sure you are well out of sight in the shadows, you pull out your lute. Several of the scoundrels, including a large ogre, have already settled down for the night. The ogre is snoring.

Softly strumming the lute strings, you hum a sad, sleepy song. One by one, the ring members nearest you yawn deeply and drop off to sleep. You sing a bit louder, and the rest of them—giant, goblins, trolls, and elves—fall into dreamland.

You and Princess Jian creep into the clearing and tiptoe to the treasure heap. As you find the ringwood sculptures, you cast them onto the closest campfire. Doe and goat, dogs and pigs, and all the rest combine to make a huge, crackling bonfire.

Suddenly you hear a sputtering grunt. You turn to see the ogre stretch and rub his eyes. Then he pulls two large wads of cotton from his ears! He did not hear your lullabies!

"What's this?" he says. "Why is it so hot here?" He sees the bonfire, but you have already grabbed Jian's hand and begun to run.

"Fire! Fire!" yells the ogre. The Magician's Ring is waking up!

You flee through the forest toward Wandelmere. Emerging from the wood, you continue to run until you see the morning sun rising over a hill in the distance.

Jian halts to catch her breath, anxiously waiting to transform. But she remains herself! The bonfire has worked! Princess Jian's auburn hair glows in the morning light.

Mevar's spell is broken for now. But you have not found the Magician. As you set off to escort the Princess safely back to the Kingdom of Wandelmere, you wonder what trickery Mevar will think of next.

THE END

from page 63

Your minstrel's interest in song-gathering is sparked, so you decide to listen to the children's game before you enter the tower. They are singing a tune that is unfamiliar to you. But you recognize some of the words:

> *Mevar has bewitched Ringdell*
> *So heed the story we will tell.*
> *'Tis not a finger ring you seek,*
> *But 'tis a ring used by the meek.*
> *You will find it if you choose*
> *The kind of ring a baby chews.*
> *If you care, if you dare,*
> *You must seek the dragon's lair!*

The children catch sight of you and run away. You wonder if their song is true.

If you now want to climb the tower, turn to page 39.

If you decide to leave Ringdell to search for the dragon's lair, turn to page 48.

from page 38

___

You decide an immediate attack is your best defense.

Gripping the cudgel like a bat, you spur your horse to turn and gallop at the goblin. You plan to knock the bow from the goblin's grasp as you charge by. But the bandit is swift, and he lets loose his arrow just as you swing your cudgel at his bow.

Suddenly everything seems to move in slow motion. Pulled by the weight of your swinging cudgel, you twist away from the robber-goblin. Then you lurch to one side as the goblin's powerful arrow drives through your rucksack and pierces your shoulder. Your horse rears in fright as the force of the blow sends you falling to the ground. You roll to one side of the path, your head spinning.

"Ho, ho!" scoffs the robber-goblin. "That will teach you to challenge a member of the Magician's Ring!"

You watch in stunned horror as he deftly lassoes your struggling horse.

"Don't try to follow me or I'll finish you off!" says the bandit. Dragging the horse behind him, he plunges into the forest and is soon lost from sight.

You are still dizzy and your shoulder throbs. But your wound is not serious. You think about the goblin's words. Is the Magician's Ring a ring of villains and thieves?

From the darkening forest comes an ear-splitting whinny—the horse!

Has he escaped? Or is he still a prisoner? Should you stay where you are so he can find you again? Or does he need your help? With a shiver of fear, you remember the goblin's threat to "finish you off!"

If you venture into the shadowy forest, turn to page 51.

If you remain where you are, turn to page 64.

84

You decide to examine the lion's ring of flames. Tamerlane has left the Big Top, but the lion's cage still covers the center ring.

The spotlights shift to attract the audience's attention to the right and left rings, while in the center stagehands in overalls heave on ropes and pulleys to raise the empty cage to the top of the tent.

The lion's ring does not look very magical without its mane of flames. You watch as a stagehand carries the ring to a shadowy corner of the tent, where it takes its place among countless other props.

There is plenty of noise and commotion as the circus continues, so you are able to sneak to the prop area unobserved.

The lion's ring stands on a metal base, and you can just reach its bottom edge. You run your hand along its surface. The ring is grooved to hold a wick of some kind, probably a rope soaked in kerosene. The charred and smoke-blackened metal leaves a smudge on your palm.

Climbing onto a crate, you are now level with the ring. You poke one of your fingers through the circular space to see if anything happens. You don't feel a thing, so you try your hand, then your whole arm. Nothing magical occurs. Finally you jump through the ring, landing on the floor beyond.

"Practicing to be a lion?" says a gruff voice behind your back. "I'd like to see you do that when the fire is lit!" It is one of the stagehands. He is resting in the shadows, waiting for the next act to end.

"Yessir," he continues, "that Tamerlane could train you to do it. He can make *anybody* do *anything,* man *or* beast! He's a strange one, all right." The stagehand shakes his head in wonder. "I'd get out of here if I were you. Tamerlane doesn't like anyone fooling with his props. Besides, I've got to take this thing apart. We'll be moving out at dawn."

The stagehand dismantles the lion's ring in a few practiced motions. The base collapses, the ring snaps into four sections, and the whole apparatus fits neatly into the wooden crate.

This couldn't be the ring you are looking for, you decide. But it sounds as if Tamerlane could be Mevar!

You spot the mysterious animal trainer on the other side of the Big Top. He has shed his whip and helmet, and is looking through a key ring attached to his belt. He strides through an exit to the fairgrounds.

If you decide to follow Tamerlane, turn to page 114.

If you take this chance to examine the seals' ring, turn to page 10.

Your head is throbbing. Now that you are sitting down, you notice how tired you are.

"Let's get some rest," you tell the Princess. "I'll unpack the apples, and clear a place to build a campfire. Then we can roast the nuts for our supper."

"I'll gather wood for the fire," says Jian. "I'm sure I won't have to look far. If you'll hum a tune for me, I'll be able to find my way back here in the dark."

Softly humming a ballad, you set about your work. You can hear twigs snapping underfoot as Princess Jian collects firewood a short distance away.

You launch into a spritely march, singing aloud and tapping your feet in time. A few minutes pass. The Princess is certainly taking a long time to pick up a few pieces of wood.

Has something gone wrong? Pausing to listen, you hear twigs and branches breaking, as though someone was running. Then you hear a scuffling noise, and an armload of wood dropping to the ground!

"Princess!" you shout. "Princess Jian!" You grab your cudgel and run ahead, but all is still. The dark, silent forest yields no clues.

Has the Princess been captured? She could be in Mevar's clutches right now!

You have no choice but to search for the magician's hide-out.

Turn to page 99.

Your path takes you through a piney wood, pleas-ant-smelling and still. It will soon be nightfall, and you'll need a place to camp. You sense no danger, but you have the odd feeling of being watched. There is no one in sight, but as you walk, the feeling grows stronger.

The best thing to do, you decide, is to prove you are friendly. You build a small campfire in the next clearing. Strumming your lute, you sing softly into the night.

Soon you have an audience of woodland crea-tures, deer and squirrels and birds. You think you spot a gnome hiding behind a bush for a chorus or two, and you are quite sure there are elves about. But you sense someone else nearby, someone with large, gentle eyes, watching and listening.

You are patient. And finally you see her—a uni-corn as white as shining snow. She is more beautiful than any creature you have ever seen. Her eyes are huge, and of the deepest pink. Her mane curls in ring-lets like wisps of palest cornsilk. Her proud horn spirals from her forehead. And at its base there gleams a golden ring!

Quietly the unicorn enters the clearing and takes her place among the other animals, as though you have been meeting for years. You are honored by her trust and do not interrupt your song, a ballad of a beggar's love for a lady fair. On and on you sing.

Your mind is racing. Could the unicorn have the Magician's Ring? Surely such a beautiful creature would not lend her powers to Mevar! But what if she is enchanted, like the citizens of Wandelmere? You don't want to frighten her away, and you know her horn can be deadly.

"*I mean no harm, my lady,*" you sing, composing as you go, "*but of the ring you wear—can this be the Magician's Ring? The Ring of cruel Mevar?*"

The unicorn does not answer. She is sleeping peacefully among the other animals, all of them sound asleep. You stop playing your lute.

If you try to remove her golden ring, turn to page 52.

If you decide to rest and see what morning brings, turn to page 92.

90

from page 24 / from page 61 / from page 75

You decide to go to the three-ring circus in the Big Top. Inside, a band is playing and the show is already in progress. You climb onto a bleacher and take a seat.

Acrobats are making a human pyramid in the left ring. To the right are clowns. And above the center ring a dainty aerialist balances on a high wire.

Suddenly, a ringmaster in a bright red coat strides into view. He blows a shrill note on a silver whistle, and the band falls silent. Could he be Mevar?

"Ladies and gentlemen," he says, "please direct your attention to the center ring." All other lights dim. "Presenting Tamerlane, the Master of Animals. He has captured arctic seals from the icy north! He has tamed the King of Beasts from the deepest jungle! The Great Tamerlane!"

The ringmaster retreats, and the crowd greets Tamerlane with cheers. He is a giant of a man, dressed entirely in furs. Waddling behind him is a line of barking seals.

The audience laughs as the seals climb onto platforms, clapping their flippers. Obeying Tamerlane's clipped commands, the animals toss balls back and forth and catch funny hats on their heads. In the finale, the seals juggle an enormous ring.

The ring makes a halo of color in the air as it spins faster. Suddenly it is over. Tamerlane exits with the seals.

Can the animal trainer be Mevar? Before you can climb down from your seat to follow him, Tamerlane is back. He casts off his furs with a flourish. Underneath, he wears the clothes of a jungle explorer.

A cage is lowered to enclose the center ring, and a circus wagon is backed up against one wall of the cage. Ferocious roars escape from the wagon.

Tamerlane barks an order and cracks his whip. The wagon slides open and a huge lion leaps into the cage.

The Great Tamerlane proves to be an able lion-tamer, and you enjoy his act. But once again, it is the grand finale that interests you. For Tamerlane forces the roaring lion to leap into the air and pass through a blazing hoop. A ring of flames! The audience gasps, and Tamerlane exits to thunderous applause.

If you want to examine the seals' ring of colors, turn to page 10.

If you want to look more closely at the ring of flames, turn to page 84.

If you want to track down the ringmaster, turn to page 106.

92

from page 88

You join the unicorn and the other forest animals in peaceful slumber. When you awake at dawn, the unicorn is staring at you thoughtfully.

You offer her an apple from your rucksack, and begin to sing:

> *Oh tell me please, my lady*
> *The golden ring you wear—*
> *Can this be the Magician's Ring?*
> *The Ring of cruel Mevar?*

The unicorn slowly shakes her head. She does not speak a single word aloud, but a sweet voice reaches your mind. You can hear her thoughts!

> *The golden ring I wear,*
> *Is not the ring you seek.*
> *But a ringlet of my pure, white hair*
> *Will render Mevar weak.*

"A unicorn's hair is as fine as a spider's silken web," the voice continues, "but it is stronger than iron." She tosses her head, and a thick lock of the magical hair falls from her mane into your hand. The ball of hair is as white and fluffy as a cloud, but as heavy as a golden coin.

"Use it well, Minstrel," says the unicorn. With a brief, graceful movement, she is gone from the clearing.

The day is warm as you set off through the forest. By late afternoon, the forest thins to a few scraggly pines. Soon you are traveling across a deserted stretch of grassland. There is not a house or road in sight.

The sky has turned a steely gray, bleaching the landscape the colors of bones and ashes. Gradually you see something in the distance. At first you think the gathering dusk is playing tricks on you. You see a fantastic head as big as a barn, lying in the grass like a forgotten haystack. But as you draw nearer, you see that the giant's profile—nose, mouth, chin, ears—is an illusion. The head is made up of stone slabs and pillars set in a circle. Each enormous stone is precariously balanced against its neighbor. It looks as if they all would come crashing down, were just one stone moved. But the circle seems so ancient and rugged that it would stand through an earthquake.

Suddenly the ground begins to tremble beneath your feet. You run until you are well beyond the circle of stones, and throw yourself face down in the tall, dry grass.

The tremor stops, and the stones remain standing. But a low, rumbling sound continues. It is a man's voice!

No one is visible in the growing darkness. The rising moon casts an eerie light on the ring of stones. You can make out some movement in the middle of the stone ring, and you sneak closer to listen. The voice drones:

Oh Ring give me Power,
Oh Ring give me Power,
Oh Ring give me Power,
When Moon reaches height,
When Moon reaches height.

There is a sudden blast of heat and light at the center of the Ring of Stones. A magician stands inside a blazing circle of fire. The fire casts its light on magical runes inscribed in the dirt, while smoke drifts upward.

The magician wears a simple robe of smoky gray that shimmers in the firelight. His back is to you, and he chants to the moon. You cannot see his face. But you know it is Mevar. There is a sense of evil in the air, and it is growing with the sound of the magician's voice.

Soon will be the Hour,
Soon will be the Hour
To seal Mevar's might!

You have found the Magician's Ring. But is it the Ring of Fire you must destroy? Or the Ring of Stones? And how can you use the unicorn's gift? You must decide before the moon reaches its peak.

If you try to destroy the Ring of Fire, turn to page 98.

If you try to destroy the Ring of Stones, turn to page 18.

from page 121

The golden sphere intrigues you, so you set off to your right. Soon you are circling the shining globe in search of an entrance. Your reflection follows you, squashed and rounded in the curving surface of the building.

Then, for an instant, your mirror image flattens to normal. A panel slides open to let you inside the globe. As soon as you enter, the panel slides shut behind you. You squint in the darkness.

"Greetings, Wanderer," pipes a squeaky voice. "I am Dr. Moonami, A.E., Astrologer Extraordinaire, gazer at galaxies, starer at stars, watcher of worlds."

Bowing politely, you introduce yourself to your host, a moon-faced fellow no taller than your hip. He is dressed in a loose-fitting robe that he has tucked into his belt at the sides. "For ease in climbing the ladder to my telescope," he explains.

As your eyes grow accustomed to the twilight, you can make out your surroundings. A huge telescope takes up the middle of the hall, like a monstrous black anteater sniffing the sky. Near the telescope is a table littered with measuring instruments. The vast walls of the sphere are papered with plans of the planets, astral predictions, and orbital paths. And the floor is nearly hidden in layers of charts and diagrams, as thick as autumn leaves.

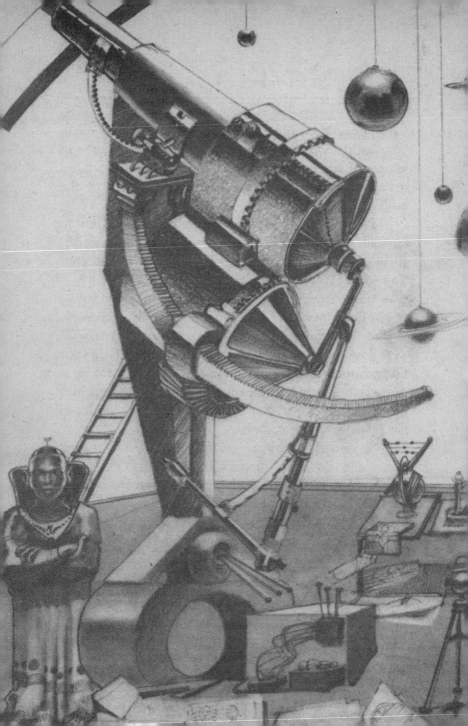

"How can I help you?" asks the astrologer. "Have you come for a chart? What is your sign? The Swimmer, perhaps? Ah, the Lute-Player, of course!"

"Dr. Moonami, I seek the Magician's Ring," you reply.

"Well, well!" Moonami's moonlike eyes get even wider. "You shall have to search heaven and earth for that! You'd best borrow my telescope while I cast your chart. Just move the lever on the side, and it will look anywhere you like."

Dr. Moonami busies himself at his worktable, and you climb the ladder to a sturdy platform beneath the eyepiece of the telescope.

If you look to the heavens, turn to page 108.

If you search the earth, turn to page 76.

from page 94

You decide to try to destroy Mevar's Ring of Fire. You will throw the unicorn's hair onto the flames and hope that its power will overcome the magician's spell.

Mevar is still chanting to the moon.

"The night is mine! The night is mine!"

You creep silently behind him until you reach the blazing ring.

"Begone, evil one!" you cry, casting the precious hair onto the fire. But the hair sizzles in the flames, and you feel the unicorn's sorrowful wail in your mind:

"Noooo, Minstrel!"

Mevar whirls about and stares at you with scorn. His face is like a lizard's, cold and smooth, but his eyes are two blazing coals.

"You waste your breath, Minstrel," he hisses, waving his hand through the ring of flame.

As if propelled by a blast of wind, you are thrown against a pillar of stone. Gray smoke swirls in your head. You hear a laugh of purely evil delight as you lose consciousness.

THE END

You press through the underbrush, hoping you can find Mevar's hide-out before any harm befalls Princess Jian.

Shadows leap at you like angry spirits, and stinging nettles scratch your arms. Fireflies blink like glowing eyes that seem to watch your every move.

Suddenly you hear voices in the forest ahead of you—low grumbles and hollow laughs.

You creep silently forward and spy through a patch of tangled briar bushes. You are looking into the mouth of a huge cave.

In the front of the cave, seated around a dancing fire, are several ogres and a snaggle-toothed troll, a gnome with a patch over one eye, a fiendish-looking elf, and the robber-goblin. They are guarding a huge pile of treasure which rises behind them.

Sitting dejectedly at the top of the pile, her knees drawn up to her chest, is the lovely Princess Jian. A thick, metal chain fastened to her wrist leads to an iron ring embedded in the rocky cave wall.

Boldly enthroned in the rear of the cave, coolly observing the scene before him, is Mevar the Magician.

Firelight plays on his cloak of glossy furs, and his hair sprouts through holes in a tortoise-shell skullcap like streams of water through a sieve. But you gaze in horror at his frightening face, half swollen and fish-like, the other side sunken like a crater on the moon. Motionless and wordless, he stares into the fire.

A burly ogre brings Jian some bread and water, but she shakes her head and refuses to eat.

"Still pining for her little minstrel, *har, har*," sneers the ogre, returning to the group.

"No worries there," says the robber-goblin. "He'll never find us. And anyway, he's afraid of Mevar! Ho, ho!"

At this they all laugh uproariously. Still the Magician does not move a muscle!

The robber-goblin waves his hands to silence his companions. You notice the flash of the ornate gold ring he wears on his finger.

"What shall we plunder next?" he asks. "There are only trinkets and a painting or two left in Wandelmere. But new riches await us in more distant kingdoms."

"First we should send the princess back to Wandelmere in the clutches of Mevar, as an example to any others who try to escape," suggests the gnome. "And Mevar could bring back the remains of Wandelmere's treasure."

"An excellent idea!" says the goblin. "Shall we vote to awaken him?"

"New riches first! New riches!" says the elf. "The princess can cook for us, and keep the cave clean."

A heated discussion follows. As the ring members argue, you notice the princess edging toward Mevar. Still he does not stir. What do they mean, awaken him? Is he hypnotized by the fire?

Suddenly you understand. Mevar does not control the Magician's Ring. *They* control *him*. The ring members create the magic!

The dispute has died down, but the thieves pay no attention to Princess Jian. They huddle together, shoulder to shoulder, chanting in a strange tongue. Then back and forth they sway, marching in a circle, snapping their fingers and clicking their teeth. Mevar the Magician begins to move! He is awake! Surely he will grab Princess Jian.

You hesitate no longer. Bursting through the briars, you slam your cudgel onto the first head you reach—the robber-goblin's!

"Ohhhhh!" he howls. "My head is ringing, ringing!"

Wham! You hit an ogre.

"It's ringwood!" he cries, and falls into a swoon.

Wham! Bam! Soon the ring of thieves is piled at your feet, holding their ears and moaning.

You look for Princess Jian. She is at the back of the cave—and Mevar's hands are around her throat!

"Stop, Mevar!" you cry, and run to the Princess's aid, brandishing your cudgel.

"Don't worry, Robin," she laughs. "I'm dragging him to the fire! See? Mevar is a puppet! Just sawdust and cloth."

"H-how?" you sputter.

"The goblin's gold ring!" says Jian. "It belongs to the crone—the Witch of Wandelmere. Quick, you must get it!"

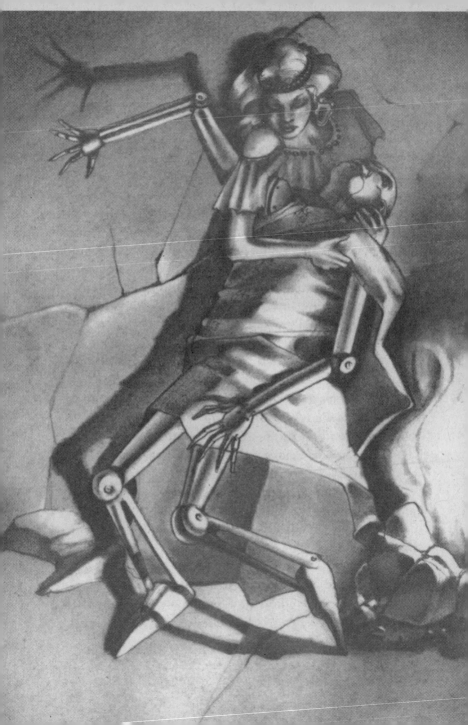

You pull the ring from the groggy goblin's finger and return it to Princess Jian.

' "The robber-goblin must have stolen the ring from the crone," she continues. "But he is not strong enough to use it by himself, so he gathered his friends together to form the Magician's Ring. Each of these forest beings has a bit of magical power. But united through the gold ring, they are powerful enough to cause a great deal of mischief!

"They created Mevar to carry out their magic spells and thievery, and to fool the crone."

You drag the puppet to the fire. It is no longer frightening. Its empty eyes stare up from its plaster face as it feeds the flames. The gnome and the ogres watch in dismay as their handiwork burns.

"What is ringwood?" you ask, examining your cudgel.

"Owww, it makes our heads spin and our ears ring!" complains the goblin. He rubs his head, on which a large lump has appeared.

You spot an iron key on an ogre's wrist. As you suspected, it unlocks Jian's chain.

As the morning sun rises over the treetops, the Princess lets out a jubilant cry. The spell is broken—she has not changed her shape!

"Let's return this treasure to Wandelmere," she says. "These creatures can do no further harm. My father will reward you well, and we have a fine tale to tell!"

You agree. You are already composing a tune, "The Song of the Magician's Ring."

THE END

from page 71

You don't want to spend the night in a cage, so you decide to sing your captors to sleep with your powerful lullabies. The guardian gnomes watch you carefully as you tune your lute, but they don't interfere.

"How about a song, fellows?" you call from your cage.

"Suit yourself, Minstrel," one answers. "You'll have little enough to sing about once Mevar gets through with you."

You decide to start with a rollicking tune, to attract the attention of the rowdiest thieves in the clearing. You launch into "The Lady Meets a Lion Wild." Soon every cur in the forest, from giant to elf, is snapping his fingers and tapping his toes in time to your merry tale. The thieves' brew flows freely, and the guards lean against logs or sprawl near the campfires.

Gradually you soften your songs, changing to deep, sad ballads. Finally you sing your slowest, most hypnotic lullabies.

"*Sleep, O sleep, like the moon on the sea,*" you croon, repeating the words until your voice is just a whisper. The last soft notes you pluck from your lute are drowned out by wheezes and snores. Your lullabies have worked!

You quickly slice through the bars of your cage with your carving knife.

"Princess Jian!" you whisper. "Let's go!"

But the Princess does not answer. She is sound asleep. You forgot to cover her ears! You shake her by the shoulders, but still she does not stir.

Leaving her to her dreams, you crawl free of the cage and sneak from one snoring bandit to the next, removing every golden ring you can find.

Then you slip back into the cage to fetch Jian, who awakens from her slumber with a start. Together you load the rings into your rucksack and flee the clearing, heading toward Wandelmere. You leave the forest behind you.

Soon the rising sun spills its pale light over the distant landscape. Your beautiful auburn-haired companion holds her breath in hope, but to no avail. She transforms once again into a sleek horse.

You empty your rucksack of golden rings, armbands and collars, earrings and toe-rings. Here, beyond the forest, they clatter to the ground.

You have escaped from the clearing, but without the Magician's Ring.

THE END

106

from page 91

You decide to keep an eye on the ringmaster, and search the Big Top for his red coat. He is nowhere in sight. But you are surprised to hear angry voices underneath you. Peering through a gap in the bleachers, you spot him directly below your seat!

He is gesturing wildly at a young circus performer, who shrinks from him in fear. She wears a sparkling white costume and a feathered plume on her head.

"What kind of bareback rider are you?" shouts the ringmaster. "What do you mean you are frightened of your horse? Can't you control your own horse? Get back to work or you know what I'll do to you!" The girl runs off in tears.

You climb down the bleachers, hoping to question the bareback rider, but she has disappeared. Instead, you see the ringmaster stomping out of the tent, his spurs jangling. Stealthily, you follow.

The ringmaster enters a circus wagon behind the carousel and slams the door. While debating whether to knock or to hide, you see the Great Tamerlane striding toward you. He walks directly to the ringmaster's wagon and goes inside. Creeping around to the rear of the wagon, you conceal yourself near a window to eavesdrop.

The ringmaster speaks first. "I've been wanting to speak to you, Tamerlane. The animals have been acting up, and it's your job to keep them in line. I hired you as an animal trainer, not for your good looks! Just remember who's boss around here!"

"Ha, that's a laugh," replies Tamerlane. "Where would you be without me? Your circus would be worthless, remember that! I can handle any animal you can name. You just manage the few performers you have left, and I'll take care of the animals!" Tamerlane stalks off in the direction of the carousel, his keys jingling on his belt.

You are confused. Has Mevar been turning circus performers into animals? Is Tamerlane the Magician? Or is it the ringmaster? And where is the Magician's Ring?

If you decide to follow Tamerlane, turn to page 114.

If you want to detour to ride the carousel, turn to page 45.

If you suspect the ringmaster is Mevar, turn to page 66.

108

from page 97

You aim the telescope at the sky. It is dusk. The evening stars swim through your vision in a blur.

You sweep the heavens, searching for a ring. Soon you find one, dancing motes of light around a mottled silver disk. It is a ring around the moon!

"Dr. Moonami, look," you say. "What can you tell me of this ring?" Could Mevar's powers increase when there is a ring around the moon? And if this is the Magician's Ring, how can you possibly destroy it?

But the astrologer laughs and returns to his work. "That is not the Magician's Ring," he says. "The Ring-around-the-Moon belongs to everyone. You must look deep—deeper still."

If you look deep into space, turn to page 122.

If you turn your gaze to the earth, turn to page 76.

from page 43

You decide to keep going, and hope to find Jian on the way. Where could she have gone? You pray she hasn't been captured by Mevar or one of his ring. Surely they would have taken both of you—unless Jian wandered off by herself. It is long past daybreak. You remember that she must be a horse once again.

The rain has stopped, but the day is still misty and gray. You hear the sound of rushing water beyond a grove of trees to your right. A brook! Perhaps Jian also heard the water and came this way for a drink.

"Jian!" you call. There is no answer.

You leave the path and head through the woods toward the watery sound. The mist is thick and the woods are gray, but the earth smells renewed and fresh as the gurgling sound gets closer.

Before you appears a silvery stream. Huge rocks rise from the mist along the stream's banks.

Cupping your hands, you take a long, cool drink from the brook. You have a jarring sensation that something is wrong.

You look downstream and see a horse's face mirrored in the rippling water. You follow the reflection to its source. It is Jian! She stands in the mist, her forelegs in the brook, her graceful neck bent down to drink. Gray and motionless, she has been turned to stone.

Your lower body is growing heavy. You look around at the other rocks. All have the shapes of animals or birds, goblins or men.

You realize that the brook is enchanted. The stony feeling spreads to your shoulders and chest, and you can no longer move.

THE END

112

You decide to follow the rolling snake. You have never seen such a creature before, and you think it may be magic.

"Thank you, Dr. Moonami!" you call, racing through the opening that instantly appears in the wall.

You find yourself on a path behind the observatory, leading away from the valley. There is no snake, but in the dust at your feet you can make out a narrow, diamond-patterned rut. A snake track?

Following the trail, you pass through a pleasant field and along the bank of a river lined with weeping willow trees. You increase your pace, for the sun is setting.

Suddenly the track at your feet takes a loop, then continues on as before. Several yards farther along, a figure-eight decorates the dusty path. A wild series of curlicues, spirals, and loop-the-loops leaves you spinning as you struggle to follow the snaking print. Finally you come to a set of lines and dots, like a path of exclamation points, as though the snake had lain down flat and then sprung onto his tail to make the dots.

"What a crazy snake!" you say, searching the dust for more tracks.

"You are looking for me, perhaps?" says a musical voice. "I am the 'crazy snake' to whom you refer."

The snake, just ahead of you, stands fully upright, balanced on the pointy end of his tail. His brilliant skin sparkles in the evening light, a jester's sequined suit.

He inclines his head toward you and flicks his tongue between his thin lips.

"I beg your pardon, sir," you say. "It's just that following your trail has left me rather dizzy!"

"I am an acrobat of sorts," replies the snake. "I run rings around most people. And you?"

"I am a minstrel by trade and I seek the Magician's Ring."

The snake eyes you suspiciously. Then, coiling like a spring, he leaps high into the air, grips his tail between his teeth, and quickly rolls away in a puff of dust.

You chase him, but come to a sudden halt at the edge of a dark lagoon. The sinking sun spills an orange streak across the inky water. The path circles around to your right, but the snake has disappeared, leaving no further trail. He must have slithered into the lagoon. A small rowboat is moored to your left. A sign nearby reads Lost Lagoon—Theater of Snakes.

If you try to cross the lagoon in the rowboat, turn to page 25.

If you keep to the path, turn to page 87.

114

from page 66 / from page 85 / from page 107

You race through the fairground, but the Great Tamerlane has vanished from sight. The circus is over, and the fairgrounds are deserted except for a few bespangled performers who straggle to their wagons.

Sniffing the air, you head for the scent of animals. You find the animal houses behind the Big Top. A large wagon, painted with scenes of arctic and jungle adventures, reads The Great Tamerlane.

Spying through a window at the side of the wagon, you watch Tamerlane pacing back and forth inside.

"What has gone wrong with the animals?" he mutters to himself. "Is there a weakness in my magical ring? Why do they rebel?"

Suddenly he turns, his eyes narrowed to angry slits. He has seen you!

You start to run, but are soon lost in a maze of animal cages. The animals begin to whimper and howl in alarm, and Tamerlane appears before you.

"So! You dare to spy on the Great Tamerlane!" he says.

"I know who you are, Tamerlane," you tell him. "You are none other than the evil Mevar, enchanter of Wandelmere."

"It is so, Minstrel," the Magician laughs. "But you shall not be able to speak it for long. Come, I need another lion!" He grabs your arm and drags you to the lion's cage.

The pacing lion roars hungrily when he sees you, and runs a dripping tongue across his monstrous teeth. He crouches, ready, in his cage.

Tamerlane removes the jingling key ring from his belt and selects a key. He fits it into the padlock on the lion's cage and the door creaks open. You struggle to pull loose from his grip, and, as you expected, Tamerlane tightens his hold on your arm. Using all of your strength, you pull him into the cage with you!

The key ring flies from his hand as Tamerlane falls to the floor of the cage. Quickly rolling to one side, you escape just as the great lion pounces. Tamerlane is trapped beneath the giant cat!

Grabbing for the keys, you leap for the door of the cage and slam it behind you. You fumble for the right key to lock the door. There is a pulsing warmth in your hand. It is the key ring!

The key ring holds dozens of heavy keys, but it is the slender ring itself that vibrates and glows. You have found the Magician's Ring! And at one point in the ring you can see a small crack. Its power is weakened!

"No, noooo!" cries the Magician. "Leave the ring alone!" Ignoring his shrieks, you twist and pull until the ring breaks with a snap, sending the keys flying in every direction.

All at once, you hear human voices. "Thank you, Minstrel," calls an enormous man from the lion's cage. It is a circus strongman, and he is sitting on Mevar's back!

From all over the fairground, men, women, and children parade by to offer their thanks. Even the wooden carousel animals regain human form and climb down from the enchanted ride.

They carry you into town on their shoulders, leaving Mevar penned inside the lion's cage.

"Hooray for Minstrel Robin!" they sing. *"For he has broken Mevar's Ring!"*

THE END

from page 38

You don't think your makeshift cudgel is a match for a well-made bow. Holding the branch across your lap, you decide to find out what the robber-goblin wants.

"Why have you interrupted my journey?" you demand. Your voice is muffled by your collar and your eyes are shadowed by your hood.

"Ho, ho!" laughs the goblin. "I meant to rob you, of course. But I see that you are in the trade yourself. A highwayman, no doubt? Your horse is so handsome, I mistook you for a nobleman."

You are relieved at the goblin's mistake. You certainly don't want to be robbed, so you decide to play along. You pull your collar more snugly over your nose and mouth, and grunt in reply.

The goblin continues to chat, seemingly glad to have company. "You won't find many victims in this wood, you know. We get few travelers here. They've all heard of the scoundrels and thieves who lurk along this pathway. Ho, ho! So tell me, highwayman, what is it you seek?"

Perhaps the robber-goblin can help you. You decide to risk the truth. Looking him directly in the eyes, you answer firmly, "I seek the Magician's Ring."

"Hoooo!" The goblin whoops with glee. "You want to join up, do you? Well, you've come to the right place. I'm a member myself!" He struts with pride.

You are confused. Join up? A member? The Magician's Ring must be an organization of some kind.

"And how do I qualify?" you ask.

"You won't have any trouble," the goblin replies confidentially. "Our members come from every branch of the trade, and skilled they are, too. We have thieves and thugs, cutthroats and curs, pirates and pickpockets, ruffians, robbers, burglars, bandits—and, of course, highwaymen. But you must meet with the master, Mevar. Come, I'll take you to our hide-out in the center of the wood."

Mevar! The name sends a chill up your back. Your horse jerks to the side, as though to pull you away. It is then that you notice an ornate gold ring the goblin is wearing on his finger. Could this be a clue to Mevar's power?

You are reluctant to go with the goblin, for your horse may change at any moment. And Mevar and his Ring of Thieves might not be fooled by your highwayman story. But if you gallop away, you might never find the Magician's Ring.

If you go with the bandit, turn to page 67.

If you decide to ride away, turn to page 28.

120

from page 55

"I would be honored to share your table, madam."

You will not be sorry, Minstrel," says the witch, serving you a bowl of dark, steaming soup. "My special broth will make you strong and quick, and will nourish you for many days."

"Why are you helping me?" you ask. You sip at a spoonful of the strange liquid and find it has a hearty flavor.

"Mevar is the enemy of all who practice magic for healing and good," replies the witch. "He has abused his magical power, spreading misery far and wide. But eat your soup, Minstrel! It will be no easy task to face the Magician. He is powerful and clever, and it is said he can change his shape at will.

"His power comes from a ring, a magical ring. Without it, Mevar is harmless. To take him by surprise, you will have to discover his hiding place, which no one has ever found. Wherever you find the ring, there you will find Mevar. *The ring must be destroyed.*

"I know but one more thing that will help you, Minstrel. *'Tis not a finger ring you seek.*"

You finish your soup and prepare to take your leave. Pushing your chair back from the table, you almost tumble over backwards. You *are* stronger!

"I thank you for your help," you tell the witch. "I will do my best."

As you set off down the road once again, your energy and confidence grow with each step. You feel as though you need but jump to sail through the air for miles. To test your newfound strength, you leap over a rock that lies in your path. Alas, you cannot fly. But you soar yards beyond the rock, landing on your feet with ease.

There is no doubt that you are stronger and more agile than you have ever been before. You spring along the road, never growing tired or breathless. By morning, Wandelmere is far behind you.

When you reach the top of a steep hill, a magnificent landscape stretches before you.

A pleasant village is nestled in a valley to your left, surrounded by fields and meadows blooming with wild flowers. The music of many chimes and bells rings across the valley from a slender tower at the center of the village.

To your right in the distance, a single round building perches on a huge rock overlooking the valley. The building is golden like the sun, and the earth and clouds around it are reflected in its curving walls. A long, narrow tube extends from an opening in its roof, pointed up at the sky. Could it be some kind of telescope?

If you investigate the village, turn to page 62.

If you visit the golden sphere, turn to page 95.

from page 108

You look deep into space. It is growing darker, silent, empty. You scan the solar system, deeper still. Your eyes find Saturn and its rings. You cannot tear your sight from the glorious rings.

"Dr. Moonami," you whisper in wonder. "What can you tell me of *these* rings?"

"Look deeper, deeper," says Moonami, his voice far away. You can barely hear him. Your eyes are fastened on Saturn's rings, to the rhythm of the brightest ring, the ring in the center, the most hypnotic of rings.

"The central ring is called the Ring of Mevar," hisses Moonami. The astrologer dissolves into thin air and the evil Mevar appears in his place.

"What is your bidding, Master?" you ask.

THE END